This book belongs to

Olivia Fowler

Copyright © 2019

make believe ideas ltd

The Wilderness, Berkhamsted, Hertfordshire, HP4 2AZ, UK.
501 Nelson Place, P.O. Box 141000, Nashville, TN 37214-1000, USA.

www.makebelieveideas.com

Written by Rosie Greening.
Illustrated by Clare Fennell.

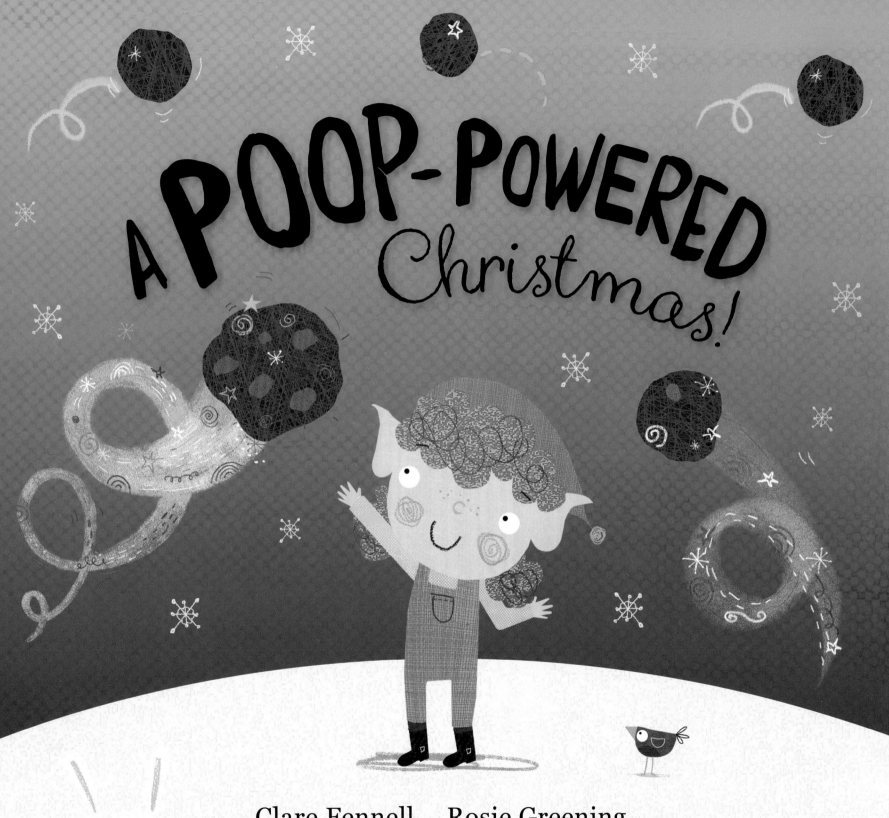

A POOP-POWERED Christmas!

Clare Fennell • Rosie Greening

make believe ideas

Ivy the elf didn't like building **toys**.

She thought it was boring and hated the **noise**.

So Ivy was given a new **job** to do . . .

... clearing up **POOP** from the big, reindeer crew!

But **poop** from the reindeer
who flew Santa's sleigh
did not seem to act
in the **typical way**.

It **whizzed** through the air with a big, **stinky**

WHOOSH,

and spiraled around with a **foul-smelling**

SWOOSH.

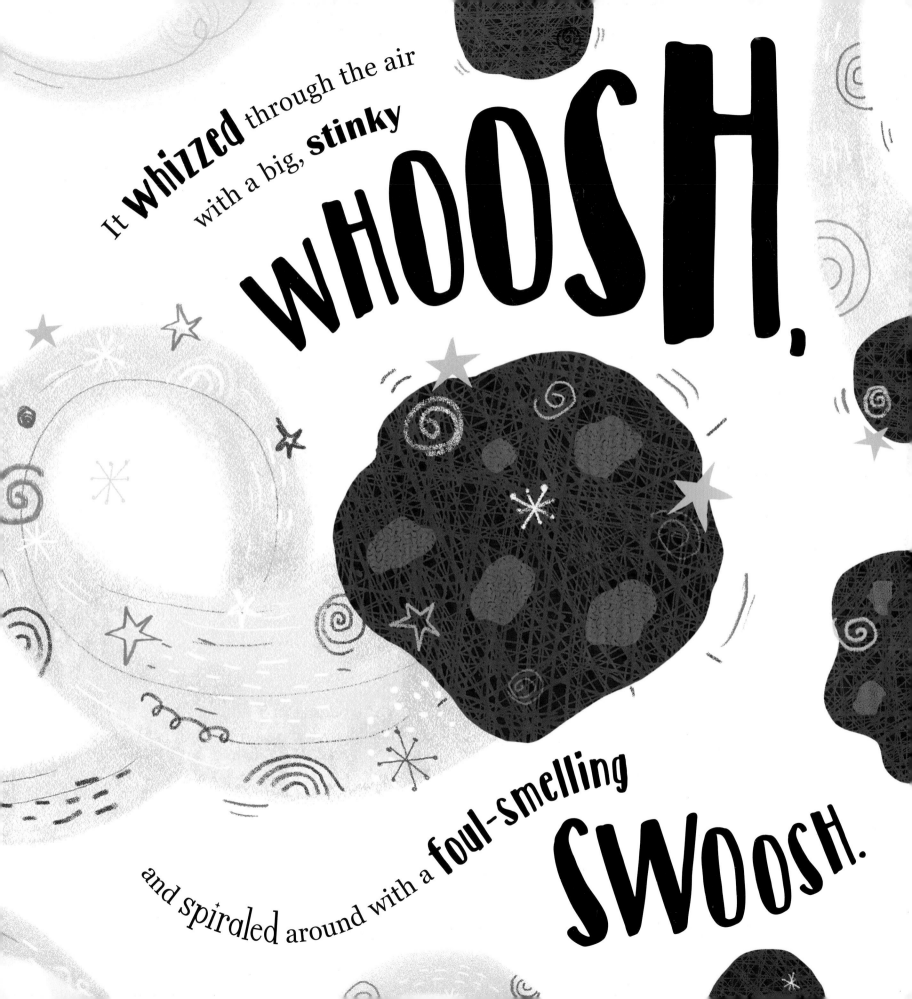

"This **poop** must be magic!" thought **Ivy** one day.

"I'll tell all the **others** and see what they say."

But the elves didn't listen;
they giggled instead.
"Who cares about **poop?**
We're too **busy!**" they said.

So Ivy just secretly **stored** it away, thinking the **poop** might prove **useful** someday.

Then one Christmas Eve, as snow filled the skies,
Ivy checked on the **reindeer** and got a **surprise**.

The reindeer were **coughing**
and **sneezing** . . .

AAAA

ATCHOOO!

The team had all **sadly** come down with the **flu!**

Dasher

Dancer

"**Oh no!**" cried out Ivy. "Today's Christmas Eve. Without you, the sleigh won't be able to **leave!**"

Prancer

She gave them some **SOUP** and then off Ivy ran
to tell all the elves that they needed a **plan**.

The head elf named Star called a **meeting** that day. She said, "We need something to power the **sleigh**."

The elves got to work: there was no **time** to lose!

But with no magic **reindeer**, just what could they use?

First, they put **sprouts** in the sleigh's **giant** tank.

But it **didn't** start flying:
it turned **green** and **stank**.

Next, all the elves **stuffed** the sleigh full of **snow**.

I KNOW!

It made nice ice cream, but it still wouldn't go.

So the **team** tried out

candy canes, tinsel, and **fudge**,

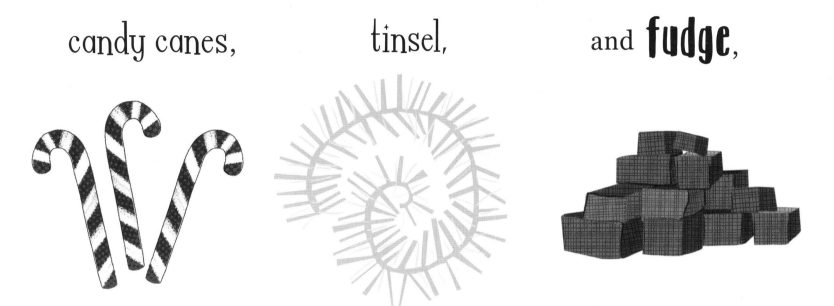

but it just made a **mess**, and the sleigh didn't **budge**!

"It's simply **no use!**"
said the head elf in fear.
"The **sleigh** still won't fly
and we're out of **ideas.**"

At last, Ivy **shouted,**

"Hey, LISTEN TO ME!

I think I know **something** that might hold the key . . ."

She led them outside to her secret trapdoor.
She whipped up the **hatch**,
and they watched the poop SOAR!

"**Reindeer poop floats**,"
Ivy cried out with glee.
"This magical **muck**
simply must be the **key**!"

They **filled** up the sleigh and then gathered around, and with one **smelly**

POP!

the sleigh **zoomed** off the ground!

The elves all **high-fived** as they shouted, "Hooray! Three cheers for Ivy, who saved Christmas Day!"

That night, they all watched Santa **whoosh** through the sky,

as the **poop** in the tank
made the **stinky** sleigh fly.

But Ivy was not with the rest of the crew.
The **head elf** had given her something to do . . .

She was down in the stable
and **testing** to see

how much magic power

was in reindeer

PEE!